# The ADVENTURES of Kirra & Rincon

## Warm Winter Waves

by **Shelley & Justin Kerr**

illustrated by **Rick Hemphill**

*The Adventures of Kirra & Rincon, Warm Winter Waves*

Published by Kirra & Rincon Enterprises, Atascadero, California

Text copyright © 2012 by Shelley & Justin Kerr.
Illustrations copyright © 2012 by Rick Hemphill.
All Rights Reserved.

No part of this publication may be reproduced in whole or in part, stored in a retrieval system, or transmitted in any form by any means, electronic, mechanical, photocopy, recording, or otherwise, without the prior written permission of the publisher, except as provided by USA copyright law.

ISBN 978-0-9766408-2-0
First Edition (2012) Printed in Korea

This book is a collaboration between Kirra & Rincon Enterprises and Laughing Pencil Studio.
Book design and pictures by Rick Hemphill—www.laughingpencil.com.

The text of this book is set in **Gorilla Milkshake**, created by Nate Piekos—www.blambot.com
The illustrations are rendered in gouache, colored pencil, and ink on Strathmore 400 Vellum Bristol.

KIRRA & RINCON ENTERPRISES · ATASCADERO, CALIFORNIA

Gazing at the pages,
Of a surfing magazine.
Excited to explore,
All the surf spots that he's seen.

Rincon's traveling to Hawaii,
Kirra's going to meet him there,
They plan to surf warm winter waves,
And relax without a care.

Leaving California's cold winter waves,
    With his wetsuit stored away.
He jumped aboard a cruise ship,
    Heading west from the San Francisco Bay.

An airplane is always faster,
    But a cruise ship is the place to be.
When surrounded by the sea life,
    Out on the open sea.

In the shallow turquoise waters,
    Of the Pearl Harbor Bay,
Rincon exited the ship,
    And Kirra met him with his lei.

Surrounded by tall palm trees,
    And huge ships around the dock,
They took a moment to learn the history,
    And then enjoyed a scenic walk.

To ride the waves of Oahu,
    They needed a special tool.
They'd studied the shapes and sizes,
    As if they were in school.

Standing in the shaping room,
    Their classic boards were done.
Rincon got a rhino chaser,
    Kirra, a balsa gun.

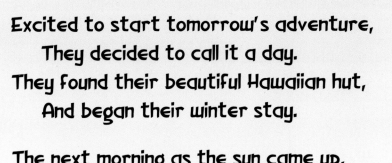

Excited to start tomorrow's adventure,
  They decided to call it a day.
They found their beautiful Hawaiian hut,
  And began their winter stay.

The next morning as the sun came up,
  They both jumped out of bed.
Rincon loaded the van with their new surfboards,
  And decided which direction to head.

They drove through the pineapple fields,
   Towards the North Shore.
They knew that the surf there
   Was what they dreamed of, and even more.

When they got to Waimea,
   They were in for quite a surprise.
The waves were so big,
   They could hardly believe their eyes.

WAIMEA
BAY →

They decided to hold back,
  And watch from the shore.
They could feel the cool ocean mist,
  And hear the loud, thunderous roar.

As each wave passed by,
  Surfers were forced to change places.
Some cutting waves, some getting tossed,
  All with excitement on their faces.

They each shared respect,
For the giant waves' power.
On the steep sandy beaches,
Under St. Peter's Tower.

Rincon had a new idea,
For something fun to do.
They could go to Hanauma Bay,
And snorkel the ocean blue.

They grabbed their snorkels and their fins,
   And ran down to the beach.
Suddenly all the marine life,
   Was well within their reach.

As they placed their faces into the water,
    A whole new world came alive.
They saw coral and fish with such vibrant colors,
    They were excited to go deeper and dive.

Gliding so gracefully through the water,
    The fish brushed against their skin.
They saw a school of yellow angel fish,
    With blue tips upon their fins.

Kirra imagined what it would be like,
To be a fish swimming through the sea.
What an exciting, beautiful place,
The underwater world would be.

As Kirra daydreamed about being a fish,
Something caught Rincon's eye.
He wasn't quite sure, but thought he saw,
A green sea turtle swimming by.

He followed the animal as far as he could,
And waved for Kirra to follow them too.
The turtle led them to a nice sandy beach,
With quite an amazing view.

As Kirra and Rincon walked up the beach,
   They found a board that had broken in two,
Something not too uncommon,
   On the golden shores of Oahu.

Coming up out of the water,
   A smiling surfer ran,
And picked up his favorite surfboard,
   One piece in each hand.

It seemed to them, a broken board,
    Was a price he was willing to pay,
To enjoy the beautiful, blue ocean,
    On a sunny Hawaiian day.

The surfer grinned and simply said
    That it was his respect for the sea,
That allowed him to erase the bad,
    And think positively.

Admiring his humble attitude,
    Rincon offered the surfer his new board.
Such a great outlook on life,
    Was hard to be ignored.

Rincon sat back and watched,
    Feeling proud of his good deed.
He new it was important,
    To help out a friend in need.

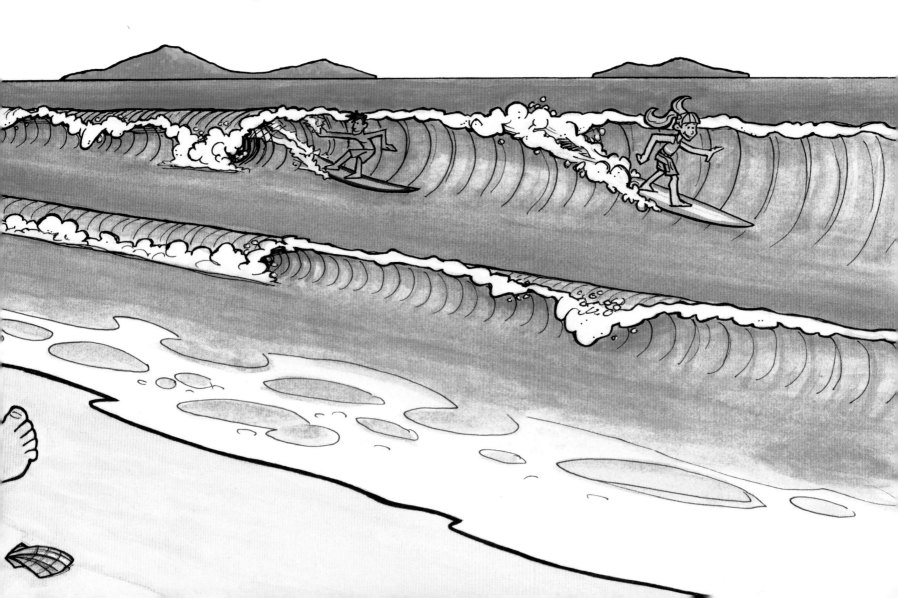

Rincon cuts back!

Rincon off the lip!

Kirra duck diving!

Kirra drops in.

As the sun began to set,
   And the day was coming to an end,
The time had come to enjoy a luau,
   With their new found friend.

The fish, the poi, the dancing,
   The music that they heard.
Made the term "Aloha,"
   More than just a word.

We dedicate this book to our three children Donovan, Taylor and Kailey. We hope the ocean plays as big a part in their life as it has in ours. A special thanks to both our parents for their contributions. Without their love and support this book wouldn't have been possible.—Shelley & Justin

PACIFIC OCEAN

KAUAI

NIIHAU

OAHU

Pearl Harbor

MOLOKAI

MAUI

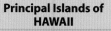
LANAI

KAHOOLAWE

HAWAII

**Principal Islands of**
**HAWAII**

SCALE 1:5,000,000
Albers equal area projection, standard parallels 8*N and 18*N, central meridian 157*W

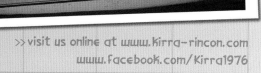

>> visit us online at www.kirra-rincon.com
www.facebook.com/Kirra1976

Dedicated to my mom who is with her Savior—I miss you! To my beautiful girls, Kiera, Brynnae, and Shaelyn, thanks for putting up with my long hours in the studio. To Becky, my amazing wife and best friend, thank you for your unconditional love and support. My ultimate thanks to God for the gift to create.—Rick

Scan this code to visit our Online store!

>> visit Rick online at www.laughingpencil.com

 Can you count how many different kinds of fish Kirra & Rincon saw while they snorkeled?